# Born a Slave

**ReadZone Books Limited**

© copyright in the text Marian Hoefnagel 2014
© copyright in this edition ReadZone Books 2017

Originally published in the Netherlands as *Als Slavin Geboren*
© 2014 Uitgeverij Eenvoudig Communiceren, Amsterdam

Translation by Isadora Goudsblom

The right of the Author to be identified as the Author of this work has been asserted by the Author in accordance with the Copyright, Designs and Patents Act 1988.

Printed in Malta by Melita Press

Every attempt has been made by the Publisher to secure appropriate permissions for material reproduced in this book. If there has been any oversight we will be happy to rectify the situation in future editions or reprints. Written submissions should be made to the Publishers.

British Library Cataloguing in Publication Data (CIP) is available for this title.

ISBN 978 1 78322 625 2

**Visit our website: www.readzonebooks.com**

Marian Hoefnagel

# Born a Slave

**FOURTEEN**

The Time of Your Life

# Contents

Difficult words have been underlined
and are explained in the glossary on page 93.

# Preface

## About the age of slavery

This is a story from the age of the slave trade, which started in the 16th century. During this time, a lot of people were transported as slaves from West Africa to America. In the 17th and 18th centuries, more and more people were taken from Africa. Millions. It wasn't until the 19th century that slavery was banned. But the human trafficking went on for a long time.

In all, 25 million people from Africa were sold as slaves. Almost half of these had already died before they got to the ship heading towards America. Twelve million people did make it to the ship. A large number of them got to America. But almost two million people didn't survive the journey. Most of them died from disease.

The largest slave traders in those days were the English. But the Spaniards and the Dutch also brought a lot of slaves to America. The French, Portuguese, Germans, Danes and Swedes were also involved in the slave trade.

**The situation in Africa**

It is often thought that slaves were caught by slave traders. With nets. The way lions are caught to be put into a zoo. But this rarely happened. It was much easier for the traders to simply buy the slaves.

The slave traders bought the slaves from African village chiefs. During that time there were many different tribes living in Africa. And they were at war with each other. The winners took the losers with them to their villages, and they used them as slaves. Then the European traders arrived. They wanted to buy the slaves. They paid the village chiefs with guns and gunpowder, with barrels filled with gin, or with beads and mirrors. Sometimes a village chief didn't have any slaves, because he had never overpowered another tribe. If he wanted guns and gin anyway, he would just sell his "own" people.

## About this story

Born a slave takes place in the 17th or 18th century, somewhere in South or Central America. Or in southern North America. Slaves were used in all of those regions. On sugar plantations, tobacco plantations, cotton plantations and coffee plantations.

Because of the free work done by all of those slaves, their masters became rich. Without slaves that would not have been possible. And so, after slavery was banned, lots of plantations went bankrupt.

The Pays and Vree plantation that is in my story never really existed. The people in my story have also been made up. But the descriptions of living conditions are true. That was what life was like in those days, if you were a slave.

The story is about three generations of slaves:
- **Shani**, who is shipped from Africa to America
- Shani's daughter **Kiesja**, who is born at Pays and Vree
- the twins **Maisa** and **Kwasi**, Kiesja's children

The story takes place during the time in which Maisa and Kwasi are fourteen years old. You will also read about earlier times – times when Shani and Kiesja were fourteen. Those pieces are in **italics**.

*Marian Hoefnagel*

# The beginning

Shani was fourteen. Only fourteen. Not yet a woman, but not a child anymore. With many others of her village, she walked through the jungle. They didn't have anything with them. No food, no drinks, no clothes. They walked carefully, one behind the other, on bare feet. They weren't scared. They were to go to a better world. That was what the village chief had said. A world without hunger, without thirst, without fear. People had already gone to this wonderful world from her village. They were waiting for Shani, on the other side of the great water.

They had to walk for a long time. Shane wanted to rest for a bit. But the white men wouldn't let her. When she stood still for a moment, one of the men immediately came towards her. He yelled something at her that she didn't understand. He picked up his black cane. 'It's a <u>fire stick</u>', Diallo said. 'Those are dangerous.' And so she walked on.

It wasn't until the sun set that they were allowed to sit down. Next to each other, in one long row.

Their legs were tied together with chains. 'They're afraid we'll run away otherwise', Diallo said. But Shani didn't understand this. Why would they run away? Didn't they want to go to that wonderful world?

Her mother had cried when they said goodbye.

'I won't see you until we reach the sky', she had said.

Shani had cried then too. 'Why can't you come with us to that wonderful new world?' she'd asked.

'I'm not strong enough', her mother had said. 'This journey is only for young, strong people. The village chief said it himself.'

Shani had hesitated for just a while. 'Maybe I would rather stay here', she had said. 'With you and the rest of the family.'

'Part of our family is already there', her mother had answered. 'They are waiting for you. And I will sleep happily every night, my child, knowing you will be in good hands there.'

The white men came by with water. And with chunks of stale bread.

'Where are we?' Shani asked Diallo.

But he didn't know either.

'Somewhere close to the great water, I think', he said.

But they weren't.  They had to walk on for days. For nights on end, they lay in the grass with their legs chained together. And then finally, finally, they got there.  The great water lay before them.

# 30 years later

Kiesja is awoken by the rooster's crowing. She needs to get up right away, like every morning. Because as soon as it is light, she has to be in the kitchen of the big white house. There, she has to prepare food for the master and mistress. And for the children. She has to prepare warm water for their bath. She has to iron their clothes. She has to ... Oh no. It's Sunday today.

On Sunday the master and mistress go to church. And then Kiesja doesn't have to get up so early. Not that she's free on Sunday. The master and mistress also need to eat on Sunday. And she of course must prepare it so that the food is ready when they get back from church.

Kiesja turns over once again on her sleeping mat.

'Are you awake yet, Nana Shani?' Maisa asks, whispering.

'No, Nana's still asleep', Kiesja whispers back. 'I'm glad she is', she adds.

Nana Shani is Maisa's grandmother. And Kiesja's mother. Nana is already quite old, older than forty. Nana has been through a lot in her life. Lots of misery, lots of pain, lots of sadness. She suffers from this a lot at night, in her dreams. She experiences it all over again: the terrible journey across the ocean, the horrible abuse.

'Diallo!' she sometimes cries in her sleep. 'Diallo, oh, Diallo.' Tears run down her cheeks.

Poor Nana Shani, Maisa thinks. My poor grandmother.

Maisa can't sleep anymore. She gets up gently from her mat and walks out of the hut. It is just starting to get light outside. Patches of fog hang between the slave village huts. Here and there Maisa sees the small light of a grease lamp. People must already be awake in the village. Maisa walks along the narrow paths towards the river. She takes a deep breath. It's lovely here, so early in the morning. The fresh smell of river water, the heavy smell of the plantation's wet, red earth.

The large wooden house belonging to the

<u>planter</u> stood by the river. It has just been painted, a fresh white. Maisa knows the house well; she's there every day. Usually she sleeps in the planter's house at night. It's much more comfortable than her mother's hut. But she prefers to sleep in the hut anyway. With Nana, with Mum and with Kwasi, her twin brother.

She slowly lowers herself into the water of the river. Not too far from the edge, that would be dangerous. The river is very deep. In the past, a lot of people have drowned in it.

When Maisa returns from her bath in the river, the women are sitting in front of the hut. Not Kwasi though, he's still lying on his sleeping mat. But that's all right, because it's Sunday. On Sunday the slaves only need to work during the afternoon.

Mama Kiesja has boiled water over the fire. She gives everyone a bowl of warm water with herbs. She does this every morning. It's Nana Shani's recipe. A recipe from Africa. 'With this drink, you can work longer' Nana always says. 'And you have to, as a slave. Especially if you're a field slave.'

*Nana Shani herself has always been a field slave, ever since she arrived from Africa. The moment she got off the ship, she was brought to the market. By the white men with the fire sticks. Other white men looked at her. They looked in her mouth, they looked at the top of her head, they felt her nearly naked body. Then they took her. She was the only one who was taken. Diallo and the others from her African village were left behind at the market.*

*She called their names and reached out her arms to them. She cried. She was afraid to go with the strange white men. She had become afraid of them. Because of what they had done on that dreadful ship. 'I'm going to look for you, Shani', Diallo called. 'I'll come for you.' These were the last words she heard in her own language.*

*Shani was taken straight to the plantation, together with a few others who had been bought at the market. All of them black girls and boys she didn't know and couldn't understand.*

*Nana Shani had to get back onto a boat. A small boat this time, a river boat. The white men showed them how to row. But it was quite difficult. Every time she did it badly, she was whipped. As were the other black boys and girls. If they screamed in pain, they were beaten again.*

*By the evening they all had bleeding <u>gashes</u> on their backs. After hours of rowing, they arrived at the Pays and Vree plantation. Nana was glad they could get out of the boat. She has never been on a boat since.*

'Did you sleep well, Nana?' Maisa asks.

Nana takes a sip of the warm spiced water. 'It was all right last night', she answers. 'Diallo's spirit was with me. He's ready to go to our ancestors. But it will be hard for him to get out of the river. We'll have to help him with lights.'

Maisa understands only half of what Nana means. Diallo, her great love from Africa, died a couple of weeks ago. Maisa knows this. He drowned in the river. Nana had been told by slaves from the nearest plantation. They had heard it from slaves of another plantation next to theirs. And they had heard it from slaves nearest to them. 'Bad news often travels faster than fire', Nana often says. And it's true.

Nana wanted to go to see Diallo's body, of course, to say goodbye. It was with him that she had left her African village. Searching for a better world. They had never found that better world. And they had even lost each other. Diallo was sold to a different plantation on the other side of the river, so they couldn't visit each other. Every now and then Nana heard something about Diallo, from slaves on other plantations. That he had tried to escape but had been caught by the soldiers and punished severely by his master. And after that he had tried to escape another time. Nana listened to those stories with a smile. Diallo did as he had promised. He was trying to come back to her. Nana wasn't allowed to go to her old friend's funeral. The supervisor did not approve.

'Slaves belong on the plantation', he said.

'You know this very well. Because you've been here for so long. This is your place in the world and this is where you'll stay. Until the day you die.'

Nana hadn't responded, of course. She knew what would happen if she did. Despite her old age, the supervisor would get out his whip. And beat her.

She didn't mind that too much.. But to get to Diallo's plantation, she would have had to get across the river. In a boat.

Instead, Nana had burned spices by the river. In the smoke that curled up, she whispered her sacred words. Nana couldn't explain which words these were. 'They are words from my own language', she said. 'I can't translate them.' Every evening Nana would burn the spices and whisper the sacred words.

And last night, Diallo's spirit had come to her. He had finally heard her words.

'What do you want us to do with those lights

exactly, Nana?' Maisa asks.

'Show him the way', her grandmother answers quickly. 'We'll put a little grease in some coconut shells and light it. We'll float the lights like boats on the river. Then Diallo will know that he can come up.'

'But he isn't in the river anymore, is he, Nana?' Maisa says. 'Didn't they take him out?'

Nana stares into the distance. 'His soul is still down there, on the bottom', she says. 'We have to make sure he comes up. Only people who love him can do this.'

In the evening Kwasi brings a few coconut shells. A friend gave them to him, a field slave who has a coconut tree. Mama Kiesja has taken a little grease from the kitchen of the planter's house. And so, in the dark of the night, five small boats float around.

Five small lights on the big, black river. An old slave stands on the side of the river. She bows her grey-haired head and folds her hands together. 'Goodbye Diallo, my dearest', she whispers. 'We'll see each other soon. I'll come to you when

Sunday comes again. I'll make sure of it. And this time, we really *will* be in a better world.'

# Monday

Kiesja and Maisa are walking to the white house together. It's still dark out, but they don't need a lantern. The night is well lit because of the thousands of stars in the sky. And because of the moon, shining brightly over the river.

'Watch your step', Kiesja warns. 'This is the time when scorpions come out of hiding.'

'Mmm', Maisa says. She's used to her mother seeing danger in everything. According to Mama Kiesja, the river is full of dangerous fish, ready to eat your toes. And in the trees there are poisonous snakes. And from all corners of the hut a <u>tarantula</u> might just pop up. But Maisa doesn't really believe all this too much. She still has all of her toes, and she's never seen a tarantula.

'Ouch!' she cries suddenly, and grabs her foot.

Kiesja is alarmed and bends over to look. But it isn't a dangerous animal that bit Maisa. No snake and no scorpion. She just bumped her toe against a tree root. 'That would never happen to Missy

Eline', Kiesja mutters. 'She has shoes.'

Maisa bursts out laughing. 'It isn't at all nice to walk in shoes', she says.

Kiesja looks surprised at her daughter.

'Really, it isn't', Maisa continues. 'I wore Missy Eline's shoes once. Shoes don't walk at all well. It's much nicer to walk barefoot.'

'Shush', Kiesja says, and puts a finger to her lips. And she whispers, 'Imagine someone would hear you now. That someone would then know you've worn shoes! You would get the whip. You know slaves aren't allowed to wear shoes.'

Maisa shrugs. 'Missy Eline said it was all right', she says. But she says it softly.

No one is up yet in the white house. Even the house slaves are still asleep. Mama Kiesja walks straight towards the slave house in the garden.

She strikes a stick against one of the poles of the hut. 'Wake up, sleepy heads', she calls. 'The rooster already stopped crowing a long, long time ago.'

Muffled sounds arise from the hut. Kiesja laughs to herself. The house slaves are exactly like Kwasi. They never want to get up.

'Come on', she says again. 'I can see the supervisor already coming towards us.'

It isn't the truth, but it works right away. The four house slaves are outside within a few seconds.

'And now', Kiesja says. 'Back to work. Prepare a bath for the master and put out some clean clothes for him. Don't forget to polish his shoes. And cut some pretty flowers for the mistress.

The boys do as they're told immediately. Mama Kiesja is their boss. And although she would never whip them, they are still afraid of her.

Kiesja had hoped both of her children could become house slaves. House slaves have much better lives than field slaves. Of course, the slaves still have to work. But at least it's not outside in the burning heat. And the work is not so heavy either.

One day she went to ask. She stood there with her legs trembling. Because slaves, of course, aren't allowed to ask questions. But she hoped that master wouldn't get angry. He did, after all, have a special relationship with Kiesja's twins.

But master didn't want Kwasi.
'He's too black, Kiesja', Master said. 'But I'll have Maisa. As a slave for my daughter Eline. It will be a nice birthday present for her.'

Kiesja thought it was dreadfully unfair, but she couldn't say anything. Slaves must do what their masters want. And so Kwasi went to work on the plantation. In the burning heat. All day, from sunrise to sunset. Six full days during the week. And half a day on Sunday.

Fortunately, Kwasi is a strong boy. Kiesja makes sure he gets enough food every day. The supervisor doesn't give the slaves all that much. A few bananas and some cassava soup. It isn't enough for the hard work the slaves have to do. But Kiesja is often able to take some leftovers from the kitchen.

And they have their own patch of land, of course. They grow <u>tajer</u>. And there are two chickens and a rooster. That way there's always some extra food.Kwasi gets most of this. Because he does the heaviest work.

*It was very different for poor Shani. She had to work on the plantation without extra food. She got only the food that all slaves got: a few bananas and some cassava soup. She worked the land for the planter for twelve hours a day. She made sure the sugar cane grew well. So that it could be made into sugar. This sugar was sold for a lot of money in town. To the white men with their large ships. They took the sugar to Europe. They came with slaves. And left with sugar.*

*Shani was made to live in a hut with an old black man with one leg. When it was light, she had to work on the plantation. When it was dark, she had to take care of the old man. And she had to have his children. Tau, was the old man's name. That's what he said, and that's what she understood. But she didn't understand the rest of what he said.*

Only after some weeks was she able to understand a little of what Tau was saying. He was a saltwater Negro, just like her. He had also travelled across the great water in one of the dreadful ships.

Shani tried to do everything right. Because she was terribly afraid of the supervisor's whip. When she was on the ship, the white men hadn't beaten her. Because she hadn't been sold yet.An unblemished slave is worth more money than a whipped slave. But in the boat towards the plantation, the beating began immediately. And it continued on the plantation. Every time she did something wrong, a beating followed. And if she screamed another one came. Until she did everything right and kept her mouth shut. After a couple of weeks the skin on her back looked horrible. Covered in scabs from old beatings. Covered in blood from the new ones.

Tau was good to her. Because he only had one leg, he couldn't work in the fields.
He fixed the tools that belonged to the other slaves.

He fixed their huts. And he picked medicinal plants and herbs for his Shani. Which he boiled in water. And in the evening he rubbed her back softly with this water. He mumbled sweet words, while doing it. It helped. And Shani was happy to be living with this old man.

She did her best, but soon Shani couldn't handle the heavy work anymore. One day she fainted. The other slave women brought her to the supervisor.
'She's pregnant, boss', the women said. 'She can't work this hard. Or she'll lose her child.'

After that Shani didn't have to work so hard. The supervisor had to be careful with his pregnant slaves. Because a slave's child meant another slave. For no cost.

So instead, Shani prepared cassava soup for the slaves to eat. She baked bananas. She looked after the children of the other slave women. And Tau taught her where to find medicinal plants and herbs.

*It was still a hard life. A life far from home,
without a family. A life amongst people to whom
she couldn't really talk properly. A life without
Diallo, who she had hoped to marry. A life with the
child of a strange man in her belly. Oh well, she had
experienced worse. Much worse. The Pays and Vree
plantation might not be heaven, but it certainly
wasn't the hell of being on the ship.*

'Will you stay and sleep in front of my door
tonight, Maisa?' Eline asks. 'I'd like that. I was
pretty afraid last night, alone like that in my room.'

Maisa bows her head. She knows that Missy
Eline won't be difficult. They've known each other
for so long. From when they were five years old.
But she still doesn't dare to look at her. Because
slaves aren't allowed to do this.

'If you wish, Missy', she says gently, with her
head down.

'Yes, I do', Missy Eline answers.

It wouldn't occur to her to ask Maisa if she
would mind. If Maisa would rather go to the
hut, to her family. She wouldn't understand that
anyway. The mattress in front of the door of her

room is nice and soft. The food from the kitchen of the planter's house is delicious. Why would Maisa want to go to that shabby hut anyway?

Maisa sneaks into the kitchen for a moment. Missy Eline is playing piano in the reception room. And Maisa isn't allowed in there.

'I'm staying here tonight, Mama Kiesja', she says.

'Are you forgetting about us?' her mother asks a little enviously.

'No Mama Kiesja, not at all', Maisa answers. 'Missy Eline wants me to stay here tonight. She's a bit scared on her own.'

Kiesja nods. 'You are allowed to stay home on Saturday and Sunday nights', she says. 'With us. The other house slaves are never allowed to stay at home. But you are. I agreed on this with the master.'

'I know, but I'm afraid to say that, Mama Kiesja', Maisa whispers. 'I'm afraid that Missy will become angry or sad.'

Kiesja looks at her daughter and then strokes her smooth brown hair. 'I understand, Maisa', she says.

She would really like to say what she thinks. That it's dangerous for her beautiful daughter of fourteen to sleep in the planter's house. That she'd rather have Maisa at home, in her own hut. Safe and sound with her mother and brother. But she doesn't say it.

*Kiesja remembers exactly how it was when she was fourteen. How dangerous it was to be a beautiful girl. She helped her mother to clear the plantation ground. And with cutting the sugar cane. They worked hard. Her mother had to finish a piece of land in one week. But this was impossible, even with the two of them.*

*'It's too much, boss', her mother Shani said to the supervisor one afternoon,*

*'We can't work harder than this.'*

*The man looked at Shani and then at Kiesja.*

*'You have a beautiful daughter, Shani', he said. 'But you've spoiled her too much. Look, her skin is light brown and not black. You're keeping her out of the sun. She should get to know real life. I'll teach her a lesson.' He spat on the ground and moved to grab Kiesja by the arm.*

Kiesja had no idea what the man meant. She looked anxiously at Shani.

'You won't get my daughter, boss', Shani said. 'We'll work until next Sunday morning, and it will be finished then.' And she went to stand in front of her daughter.

The supervisor's eyes widened with rage. 'A slave who contradicts me?' he yelled. He grabbed his whip and started to beat Shani horribly. Not on her back, like he always did with <u>disobedient</u> slaves. But on the front of her body. Even on her face.

Shani screamed. Kiesja screamed. The supervisor yelled. Slaves came walking towards them from all sides. And suddenly Master was there too, on his horse. Master himself! 'What is going on?' he asked, surprised.

All of the slaves looked down at the ground. The supervisor stopped the beating. Only Shani stood with her head up, looking at the master. The blood was streaming all over her face. She said nothing.

'Go to your hut, woman, and take care of your wounds', was all Master said.

Tau washed Shani's wounds and shook his head. He had never seen such deep gashes. And he had seen many lately. This supervisor was new and had to prove himself. Which he did by using his whip as often as he could, even when nothing was wrong. But it was obvious that there had been something wrong now.

Will you tell me why you've been beaten so, my Shani?' he asked.

'He wanted Kiesja', Shani said. 'And I know what that means.'

'He'll get her anyway, though', Tau said.

'When a white man wants a slave, he'll get her. It wasn't wise to let yourself be beaten so badly because of it.'

'It was wise', Shani answered. 'Make me a white doll, Tau.'

Tau shook his head again. But he did what Shani asked him to do. Out of soft wood, he cut her a little doll.

*Tau and Kiesja spent the entire night sitting in front of the hut. They weren't allowed inside. Inside, Shani was muttering words from her own language.*

*Harsh words they couldn't understand. It wasn't until the morning that Shani fell asleep. Next to her lay the little doll, which was now missing his left leg.*

*The next day the supervisor was bitten by a scorpion. Everyone thought it strange. Not a single scorpion had ever been spotted at Pays and Vree before. And now the supervisor was dead in his cabin, with a dead scorpion on his left leg.*

*From that day on, Shani only had one eye. From that day on, Shani didn't need to work so hard. She was still a field slave. And the new supervisor still came by to check her work. But he didn't say anything about it if it wasn't finished. And from that day on Kiesja was allowed to work in the white house. The master himself had come to tell her. That he had decided to let Kiesja work in the kitchen. This was strange too.*

*'See', Shani said to Tau in the evening. 'It was very wise what I did. My daughter is going to be a house slave. She's going to have a better life.'*

Maisa always sleeps very well on the mat in front of Missy Eline's door. It's nice and cool on the first floor of the white house. The wind blows through the open veranda from across the river. And the horrid insects that sting so much don't get up this high. They prefer to stay close to the ground. She doesn't need to be afraid of tarantulas or snakes here either. The house slaves check the house every day. They rub the wooden floors with oranges and lemons. That smell keeps all kinds of animals at bay. I'm lucky to be Missy Eline's slave, Maisa thinks.

As she lies on her mat, she hears the master talk to the supervisor. They are sitting in Master's study. He usually has his door closed, but not this time. The supervisor says that the slaves are restless.

'They talk a lot to each other, sir', the supervisor says.

'Then you forbid it', Master says. 'With the whip. I've heard that many slaves have run away from other plantations, into the woods.'

'Yes, sir', the supervisor answers. 'I've heard that too. But they can't survive in the woods. There are too many dangerous animals there. And they're walking barefoot! I think the runaways will come back again soon.'

'Or we'll send soldiers to get them', Master says. 'We just let slaves walk away, of course.'

It's quiet for a while. Then the supervisor says: 'I know who is telling the slaves to run away. It's Gamba. His wife died recently in childbirth. Gamba thinks it's my fault, because I beat her too much. That's why the child was born too early, he says.'

'You beat a pregnant woman?' the master asks surprised.

'No, no, sir, of course not', the supervisor says quickly. 'I'm always very careful with pregnant women.'

'I hope you are', Master says. 'Because I can't have one dead slave, one dead baby and a slave who's telling the others to run away!' You have to keep the peace on the plantation, man. That's what I'm paying you for.'

'Yes, s-sir, of course, s-sir', the supervisor stutters.

I'm going to have to ask Kwasi if all of this is true, Maisa thinks. Then she falls asleep.

# Tuesday

In the white house, Maisa is up early. Her mother always comes to wake her. So that she can help to get breakfast ready. Eggs, cornbread, fresh milk and coffee. Every now and then, bacon.

'Did you know that Master Walter is coming home in four days?' Maisa says. 'They are busy kneading the corn flour for the bread.'

'Yes, I heard', her mother answers.

'There's going to be a big reception', Maisa babbles further. 'The neighbours from the other plantations will be there. Missy Eline got a new dress. And I have to stay with her the entire night. To keep her cool. With a parasol and with a fan. And so I have to wear a dress too. An old dress belonging to the missy, I guess.'

'Mmm', Mama Kiesja says. 'I'm not looking forward to it.'

'Oh, but I'll help you with everything, too, of course', Maisa says.

'It is a lot of work, such a large party. But the

houseboys will be there, too. And maybe Nana can help out a little. And I've heard the neighbours' slaves will be there to help as well.'

'I know, Maisa', Kiesja says. 'They've been planning this party for weeks.'

'I think it will be such fun', Maisa goes on. 'It's exciting to have a party like this. Isn't it, Mama Kiesja?'

'Mmmm', Kiesja says again.

She can already see it. Her beautiful daughter between all those strange men. The white neighbours and their sons. The black neighbour slaves. Once they've laid eyes on Maisa, they'll be lining up for her. Maisa, with her beautiful light brown skin and her blue eyes. Maisa, who has no frizzy hair like all the other slaves. Maisa, who has a white father. Who looks so unique because of this. That is why Kiesja prefers to keep her daughter really close. Day and night. The fewer men that lay eyes on her, the better.

Kiesja looks to the side for a moment. It's Maisa's blue eyes especially, that strike her as strange.

Her father didn't have blue eyes. His eyes were simply brown. But it was all a bit strange how her children had turned out. Maisa, who's so light-skinned. And Kwasi, her twin brother, who's pitch-black. How is that possible?

*Kiesja isn't sure whether her father really was old Tau. She can't ask him. When she was fifteen, he passed away. Calmly, as he had lived.*

*'See you in the next life, my dear Kiesja', Tau said. 'Take good care of your mother. She did the same for you. Even though she didn't really want you in the first place.'*
*Kiesja was left a little sad. And surprised. What did Tau mean? Her mother didn't want her? Why not?*

*She asked her mother of course, when she returned from her working day.*
*But Shani didn't respond. There were certain things she simply didn't want to talk about. Ever.*
*But there were other things about which she could be quite open. How you could make sure not*

to get pregnant, for instance. Kiesja was barely twelve when she learned all about this. And she spoke about a lot of things like this with Maisa too. About herbs that can stop menstrual periods. About fruits that can end a pregnancy. 'Slaves shouldn't have children', Shani thought. After Kiesja, she hadn't become pregnant ever again.

So it was a huge shock to her, when Kiesja turned out to be pregnant. And especially when Kiesja didn't want to end her pregnancy. She wanted to have her baby. 'But you don't have a husband', Mama Shani said. 'And it will be a slave child.' Kiesja didn't care.

When Maisa and Kwasi were born, the shock was even bigger. A light-skinned child with blue eyes and a black child with brown eyes. How was this possible? What kinds of spirits were around these babies?

Nana burned her herbs again and mumbled some words from her language. But after a few weeks, she gave up. She hadn't wanted Tau. She hadn't *wanted Kiesja. She hadn't wanted Maisa and Kwasi. But she had come to love all four of them more than anything else.*

The master, mistress and Eline have just sat down at the table. Kiesja made a delicious lunch of tajer, cassava biscuits and salted meat. Suddenly a horrid scream pervades the kitchen. Kiesja knows right away it's Shani. She knows she shouldn't leave. But she runs towards the hut anyway.

When she gets to the hut, Shani is in the garden picking herbs, which she puts in a bowl. She keeps her head down; she doesn't look at Kiesja. Kiesja understands why right away. Something has happened to Kwasi. And if they look at each other, they will cry. Scared, she looks into the hut. Kwasi is on the floor with his back turned towards her. Bleeding gashes run from the left to the right of his back.

'Oh, son', Kiesja whispers. 'Are you in a lot of pain?'

She doesn't ask what happened. Because it doesn't matter. Kwasi was beaten. That's all there is to know.

Kiesja walks sadly back towards the white house. Nana will take good care of Kwasi. But she'd much rather be with him herself right now. All her thoughts will be inside the hut for the whole afternoon. Not in the kitchen of the planter's house.

Kiesja has to wait until the evening to hear what happened. Gamba had been hung from the branch of a large tree. Upside down. The supervisor had shouted that he was a troublemaker. That he made brave slaves walk away, into the woods. That he was to be punished because of this. He had whipped poor Gamba terribly. Afterwards he had taken the whip and given it to another slave.

'You have to beat him, too', the supervisor said. 'Or I'll beat you.'

The slave did it. He had no choice. He had tried to beat Gamba carefully.

'You have to whip him harder, man', the supervisor had said.

And this too, the slave had done. After that, all

the other slaves had to beat Gamba. One after the other. When it was Kwasi's turn, he refused.

'If you don't beat that rebel, I'll beat you', the supervisor threatened.

But Kwasi wouldn't take the whip. And so it happened. The supervisor had turned his anger towards Kwasi. Moments later Kwasi lay on the floor with terrible gashes, moaning.

'What happened to Gamba?' Kiesja asks.

'He was more dead than alive when they took him down from the branch.' Kwasi says.

'Someone has to take care of him', Kiesja says. 'His wife can't do that for him anymore.'

'Maybe you could go to him, Nana?'

But Kwasi shakes his head. 'It's pointless now, Mama Kiesja', he says. 'They've thrown him into the river.'

# Wednesday

'My son has been beaten, Master', Kiesja says. 'He's in a lot of pain. He really can't work today. Would it be all right for him to stay with his grandma?' She can heal his wounds. Tomorrow will be better; he'll be able to work again.'

Kiesja trembles while speaking these words. She finds it terribly difficult asking the master. But she still does. After all, Master is Kwasi's father. If there's anyone who can help him, it's Master.

*A long time ago, master had been in love with Kiesja. At least, that's what Kiesja had thought. A long time ago, when she was fourteen. She had just started as a kitchen slave. She swept the floor, she scoured the pans, she did the washing up. She was busy in the kitchen the whole day.*

*There had been an older slave who'd taught her everything: Binti. Binti told her she could only be in the kitchen. She was not allowed to go into the house. Binti did that herself. Binti brought the food*

*to the dining room. Binti went to clear the plates.*
*Binti made sure there were drinks on the veranda.*
*Or coffee in Master's study.*

*One day Master asked if Kiesja could come in.*
*'She's such a lovely girl, Binti, the one working*
*with you in the kitchen', Master said, 'I would like her*
*to bring my coffee sometimes.'*
*Binti bowed her head and said, 'Yes, sir'.*
*Back in the kitchen she warned Kiesja. 'When a*
*master asks for a slave, he wants something', she said.*
*Kiesja didn't understand. 'Coffee?' she asked.*
*'No, sweetheart, not coffee. He wants you in his*
*bed', Binti said.*
*Kiesja was shocked. 'Why me?' she asked. 'I'm much*
*too young.'*
*'That's exactly why', Binti said.*
*'What do I do?' Kiesja asked, frightened.*
*'Don't go near him', Binti said. 'That's all we can try.'*

*It worked for a couple of weeks. Binti continued to*
*bring coffee to the master. When he asked for Kiesja,*
*she would say: 'Kiesja is working now. She really*
*can't come.' But after a while the master*

*said it was enough.*

*'I want you to send Kiesja to me right now', he said. 'Or I'll go and get her myself.'*

*And then Kiesja had come in. Shy, scared.*

*'Just put the coffee down here', Master had said. 'On the side table next to my chair. And come sit with me for a bit, sweetheart.'*

*Kiesja sat down on the floor next to him. But master wanted her on his lap.*

*'You're such a pretty girl', he whispered. 'So pretty, so pretty.'*

*He had stroked her hair and her shoulders. He had kissed her gently, on her cheek. Then he asked her whether she was afraid of him.*

*'A little bit, sir', Kiesja said.*

*'You don't have to be, sweetheart', Master said kindly. 'I will never, never hurt you. I promise. I love you, do you know that?'*

*Kiesja had shaken her head. 'No, sir.'*

*'Now go back and help Binti again, sweetheart' Master said. 'And tomorrow, come and bring me my coffee again.'*

*Kiesja slipped off his lap. 'All right, sir. Thank you, sir.'*

*This continued for a few weeks. Master kept being very nice. He whispered kind words. He stroked her shoulders. That was all. Occasionally he would fondle her breasts. And sometimes he asked her whether she loved him too. And Kiesja would simply say, yes. Sometimes she thought it might even be true. That she loved him too.*

*One day Master said, 'Look at me, Kiesja.'*
*Surprised, Kiesja turned her eyes towards him. She had never looked straight at a white man. She saw two friendly brown eyes. A white face with narrow lips. And a red moustache. The red moustache came in closer. Then master kissed her on her forehead.*
*'There, sweetheart', he said. 'Now, the time has come. Get undressed and lie down on the <u>divan</u>.'*
*Kiesja was shocked. This was it. It was going to happen. She had asked Binti what it meant. That Master wanted her in his bed.*
*'Oh', Binti had said, 'It's a man's thing. Women*

*rarely think anything of it. But you know, it's a part of life.'*

*And so Kiesja became the master's lover.In the beginning she didn't think much of it indeed. But this changed after a while. Master was always so sweet to her. All those hours of lovemaking on the divan were actually rather pleasant.*

*Kiesja said nothing to her mother. She didn't dare. But Shani noticed when Kiesja's belly started to grow.*

*'Are you pregnant?' she asked, with a frown.*

*'I think so, Mama Shani', Kiesja said, trembling.*

*'Whose is it?' Shani asked angrily.*

*'Master's, Mama Shani', Kiesja whispered.*

*'I have to bring him his coffee every afternoon. He doesn't want Binti to do it anymore.'*

*'But you know what to do!' Shani said. 'You know the fruits and the spices to use. Don't let this child be born, Kiesja!'*

*'I want to keep it, Mama Shani', Kiesja said quietly. 'I love my baby.'*

*Shani sighed. 'You're not going to tell me you love the baby's father, too, are you?' she said.*

*Kiesja bowed her head. Tears trickled onto the floor.*

*'I do', she said. 'He's very kind to me. And he says he loves me.'*

*Shani shook her head. 'He loves you when you're in his bed, Kiesja', she says. 'The moment you get out of it, he's already forgotten you.'*

*'He loves me', Kiesja insisted. 'And I think that he'll love my baby too.'*

*But unfortunately that wasn't the case. As soon as the master knew that Kiesja was pregnant, she wasn't allowed to come in again. And he didn't want to know anything about her children.*

Master looks up from behind his desk. 'Your son has been beaten?' he asks. 'Oh, Kiesja, I'm so sorry. I'm sure you raised him very well. And that he knows how to behave himself.'

'Yes, sir', Kiesja mumbles. 'He's always been a good boy.'

'Then the supervisor must have made a mistake?' he asks.

'I don't know, sir.' Kiesja says carefully. 'All I know is that my son is in a lot of pain. And that he really can't work today.'

Master looks at the slave. She's still a beautiful woman. Not as pretty as her daughter, Maisa, but still, a beautiful woman. If she hadn't had children, she would have still been his lover. He's sure of it.

But a mistress with children? No, he didn't want that. That was all too complicated. Like now. Kiesja asks this of him because she thinks he's Kwasi's father. He understands this all too well. He has always thought he might be Maisa's father. But not Kwasi's. He thought Kiesja must have had had another lover. A black lover. And that she got pregnant from both of them.

'I understand your son is a strong boy', he says, friendly.

'Yes sir, he is', Kiesja answers.

Then I'm sure he can handle a beating or two, Master thinks. 'He has strong, black skin', he says. 'His wounds will heal quickly in the sun.

I think it will be best for him to just get to work today.'

He waves his hand a little, indicating the conversation has come to an end. He really can't give Kiesja what she wants. Because then she'll ask him for something again next week. And the week after that. No, she has to understand that she's a slave and that she can't ask for anything.

# Thursday

'I'm going to come with you', Shani says to Kwasi. 'We'll do your job together. And if you're in a lot of pain, I'll put leaves on the wounds.'

'You can't, Nana', Kwasi says. 'You're too old to work.'

'You're too sick to work', Shani answers.

'We'll do it together. We can make it work.'

They walk across the plantation, both of them bent over. Nana from old age, Kwasi from pain. It's still early, but the slaves are already working.

'Go back to your hut, Nana Shani', they say. 'Both of you, you can't work. We'll do it for you.'

But Nana Shani shakes her head. 'You have enough to do yourselves', she says. 'We'll be fine.'

And they walk on, to their own workplace.

They try to clear the ground together. But it's hard work. They aren't making a lot of progress.

'Nana, I can't do it anymore', Kwasi says after a few hours. 'I have to rest for a bit.'

'That's fine, child, Nana answers. 'I'll come and sit next to you.' She gently strokes her fingertips over her grandson's damaged back. She sings while doing it. A song in a foreign language.

'Nana, I'm so unhappy', he suddenly says, sobbing. Nana is startled. She looks around in fear, but luckily no one is in the neighbourhood.
'Oh, my child', she then says. 'It's your age. Every fourteen-year-old boy is unhappy. In a few years you'll feel better. You'll have a wife and a hut of your own.'

'No, Nana', Kwasi says. 'I'll never be happy here. I hate it here. I'm a field slave! I have nothing and am allowed nothing. I can see that Mama and Maisa are all right on the plantation. But maybe that's because they're house slaves. They're allowed more because their skin is lighter than mine. I'm too black to be happy at Pays and Vree, Nana. I want to get out of here. I want to escape, into the woods. I want to be free.' Nana has never heard Kwasi speak so much in one go. She's speechless.

'I'm a field slave too, Kwasi', she says. 'My skin is just as black as yours. I have also always had to work hard. And I've been beaten too. But still, life on the plantations isn't as bad as you think it is. It can be much worse, child. Much worse. You have people around you who love you, who take care of you. You have food every day. You're safe on the plantation. The woods are dangerous, child. You don't know how to survive there.'

'The others will help me, Nana', Kwasi says. 'There are a lot of runaway slaves in the woods. Gamba told me. I want to go to them.'

'But we need you', Nana tries to insist. 'You're the only man in our hut. You have to protect us.'

Kwasi shakes his head. 'I can't protect you, Nana', he says. 'Mama Kiesja and Maisa are protected by their light skin. That's why the others are kind to them. And you are protected because you know a lot about herbs. The others respect you for that. I have nothing, Nana. And I am no one.'

Nana understands exactly what Kwasi means.

Being no one, having nothing.She shivers for a moment. Thoughts pop into her head that she had pushed far away deeply. Thoughts about the day she got on that boat ...

*The white men who shouted and pressed <u>a burning hot iron onto her back</u>. The smell of burning flesh. Other white men throwing seawater onto the wound. Even more men, who chained her legs. With that chain she was fastened to the boat. At the very bottom, in the dark. All of them lay close to each other. In rows. You couldn't turn around. Or sit up straight. There wasn't enough space for it.*

*It was cramped in there with so many people. A few hundred men lay in the bottom of the ship. And another few hundred women in the space above. Everyone was screaming or crying. Everyone was in pain or scared. Shani tried to think about the wonderful world on the other side of the water. Where her family would be waiting for her. But she couldn't really think about it. The brand on her back hurt terribly.*

*She had lost Diallo immediately. And all the others from her village too. There was just one girl she knew, Oba, lying next to her. One girl who could speak her language.*

*'I have to pee', Oba sobbed. 'What do I do now?'*

*'Just let it out', Shani said. 'I think that's the only option.'*

*'But that's disgusting, isn't it?' Oba cried. 'And what if I need to poo?'*

*'I just don't know', Shani said. 'Maybe we'll be released soon so that we can go up on deck. Maybe this is just for a short while.'*

*But it wasn't for a short while. The hundreds of slaves would remain on the ship for months. In their own stench and that of others.*

*After a week they were taken out of the hold. Shani, Oba and the other slaves who were in their row. After a week in the dark, they were back in the sunlight. It hurt their eyes.*

*The white men drew buckets of water from the sea. They threw the water over the girls and women.*

*For the first time in days they felt a little normal.*
*For the first time in days they felt like they were*
*human again, instead of feeling like beasts.*

*Soaking wet, they stood looking at each other, a*
*little giggly. Then Shani's eyes widened with fright.*

*'Oh no, Oba', she said. She pointed at Oba's legs.*
*Oba's legs were covered in sores. Dangerous sores.*

*Oba looked at them now too. Tears rolled down*
*her cheeks. Back home in their village in Africa,*
*everyone was very afraid of the ulcer disease. If*
*someone had ulcer disease, no one could touch*
*him. You had to walk around anyone diseased at*
*a distance. Because otherwise you'd get the sores*
*yourself.*

*One of the white men had seen it too. He yelled*
*something at Oba and gestured for her to come.*

*'Is he going to shoot me?' Oba asked Shani,*
*terrified.*

*Shani didn't say anything. She didn't know what*
*would happen.*

*But Oba wasn't killed. The white man took her to*

*the ship's doctor. He put a few bandages around her legs. And then Oba was brought back to her place in the bottom of the ship. It was a bit cleaner now. Cabin boys had washed away the filth.*

*The poo, the pee, the vomit. But the smell was still terrible though.*

*No one was allowed to lie to the left or right of Oba. Those places were kept open.*
*'Shani?' Oba said. 'Shani, where are you?'*
*But no one answered.*

*Shani no longer had to lie in the bottom of the ship. She was now in the galley, the ship's kitchen. One of the white men had taken her and pushed her into it. He had said something to the men in the kitchen. They all laughed.*

*One of them had made a gesture. Shani understood she was to go and stand at the stove. He had shown her what to do: cook kidney beans and barley. She had to make soup with these ingredients. It was the food for the slaves.*

It was very warm working there, in the galley. But Shani was happy she wasn't tied up anymore. That she didn't have to lie in that awful stench any longer. She did miss Oba. In the kitchen, there were only white men.

When the food was ready, she had to help hand it out to the female slaves. Every one of them received a scoop of water out of a large bucket. And a scoop of soup from a different bucket. With a piece of stale bread. The slaves were surprised at Shani. A black woman passing out food? A black woman who belonged to the terrible white men? What was this? Some of them spat at her. Others hissed threatening words. Shani couldn't understand them. But she knew what they meant.

At night, Shani slept in the kitchen, together with the kitchen boys. She was tied up again, chained to the floor. There was more room here though, compared to down there, at the bottom of the ship. But she was not happy for long. In the dark, the kitchen boys came to her one by one. They would feel between her legs and lie down on top of her.

*Shani cried out that she didn't want it, that it hurt. Shani cried and tried to push the men away. But the men only laughed. Some put their hands in front of her mouth, so that she nearly suffocated. Others kissed her on the mouth and that was even more awful. I'm going to die, Shani thought. I'm not going to survive this.*

*But strangely enough she woke up the next morning. And she had to get back to work, as always. Cooking the kidney beans, the barley. And handing out soup to the poor slaves. She tried to do the work as well as possible. Maybe I'll see Diallo today, Shani thought. And other people from my village. But she didn't. She just had to go on handing out food to the same slaves. The slaves who spat at her and hissed nasty things at her.*

*Every night Shani was raped by a few men. Every night, over and over again. She never knew who they were; it was too dark to see in the kitchen. But it didn't really matter anyhow. They were all ugly, white men with a lot of hair on their faces. With dirty brown teeth, straight yellow hair and blue eyes.*

During the day she tried not to think about it. She would focus her attention on the kidney beans and the barley. Then she would try to take care of the slaves down there as well as possible. Because she felt sorry for them. When she saw someone who was very ill, she would call for one of the white men. Sometimes the slave could then go to see the doctor.

Shani saw a lot of misery. Dead slaves, dying slaves, slaves who moaned in pain. Slaves who begged for her help, who asked for more water or food. Slaves who were so sick they couldn't eat or drink anymore. At the end of the day she had often lost her own appetite. It made her that miserable. The nights were terrible, but the days weren't much better.

One day a group of female slaves stood on the ship's deck. A bucket of seawater had just been thrown over them. The slaves screamed and shouted and were pointing at someone. Shani couldn't properly see what was going on. But then a slave started to run. She ran all the way across *the deck, to the other side of the ship. When she passed the kitchen, she saw Shani. She didn't stop, but she did look straight at Shani. Her face was completely covered in sores. So was the rest of her body. Her legs, her arms.*

*'Goodbye Shani, I can't do it anymore', she said.*

*Shani stood still. She felt her heart beating in her throat. She hadn't recognised the woman. But when she heard her voice, she knew that it was Oba. Oba ran to the back of the ship. Then she jumped over the railing and into the sea.*

*For the remaining weeks of the journey, Shani thought of Oba. Every day she remembered the image of Oba jumping into the sea. And she often thought of doing the same. At least all the misery would be over with.*

*But she didn't do it. She still hoped to see Diallo again. And that one day they would be together. In a better world, on the other side of the great water.*

Nana looks at her grandson and sighs. She can't

tell him how badly she had it on the ship. How much better life is here on the plantation. It won't make him any happier. It won't give him hope. And hope is what he needs to be able to survive.

'I understand you want to leave, child, she says. 'But don't go just yet. Wait till you're a little older. Or at least until your wounds have healed.'

Kwasi bends his head down to his knees. He doesn't answer.

# Friday

Maisa has to help Missy Eline get ready. For Master Walter's big reception.

'You can do my hair so well, Maisa', Missy Eline says. 'I want it all put up.'

'Of course, missy', Maisa says, and she starts brushing the long blonde curls.

'I'm so curious to see what my brother looks like', Missy Eline says. 'I haven't seen him for two years.'

Maisa nods.

'He's eighteen now', Missy Eline continues. 'A man already. Remember how we used to play together, once?'

'Yes, missy', Maisa says.

She remembers it well. The three of them were always together. They played the games all children play: hide and seek, marbles. They swam in the river. It didn't matter then that Maisa was a slave. Missy Eline and Master Walter would go to school. When they got home, they would keep on playing. And they taught Maisa to count and write. Because Maisa wasn't allowed to go to school.

School was only for white children.

'At last, there's my beautiful sister! Master Walter is standing in the doorway, with a big grin on his face.

'Walter!' Missy Eline yells, and she flies up from her chair. The hairbrush still stuck in her hair.

'Easy, easy! I'm going to be here for a while', Master Walter says laughing. He wraps his arms around his sister and kisses her on her forehead.

'Oh, it's so nice to have you here!' Missy Eline cries. 'You'll dance with me tonight, right, Walter?'

'Of course not' Master Walter teases. 'You're much too small for that, sis.'

'That's not fair', says Missy Eline and pretends to cry.

Master Walter laughs. 'All right, I'll dance with you once', he promises. 'But then I must dance with the lovely Maisa, too. He looks at Maisa, who looks politely at the floor.

'Don't even think about it', Missy Eline says angrily.

Maisa looks up, surprised. She's never heard Missy Eline talk to her brother like this.

'Maisa is my slave, Walter', Eline says. 'You'll keep your hands off her.'

'Well, well, take it easy', Master Walter says. 'I'm your brother! Am I not allowed to borrow Maisa from you for a couple of minutes?'

'No', Missy Eline says loudly.

Master Walter chuckles and strokes his sister's blonde hair. 'I was joking, Ellie', he says softly. 'You can't possibly think father would let me dance with a slave?'

Missy Eline's cheeks turn red. But she says nothing.

It's a busy evening at the planter's house. All the neighbours have come to welcome Master Walter home. They bring their own sons and their daughters. There is eating and drinking. There is music and dancing.

Missy Eline looks stunning. She's wearing a new blue dress with a big bow. She wears a matching blue bow in her hair. She also has new shoes. And a blue bag that matches her dress.

'You have to stand or sit next to me the whole time, Maisa', Missy Eline had said. 'Everybody must see that I have my own slave.'

And so Maisa learns who all the white neighbours are.They don't shake her hand, of course. They don't ask for her name, of course.

Every now and then someone says, 'What a luxury, Eline, your own slave. And such a pretty one, too.'

But no one says anything directly to Maisa.

Except Master Walter. When Maisa and Missy Eline walked into the reception room, he came towards them.

'You look lovely, sis', he told Missy Eline. 'And so do you, Maisa', he added.

Maisa had said softly: 'Thank you, sir.'

She thinks she looks rather pretty herself. She's wearing an old yellow dress of Missy Eline's. Of course she's not wearing any shoes. Nor a bow in her hair. But she can see that many people are looking at her.

Missy Eline plays a few songs on the piano; she's good at that. The guests applaud her and call out, 'Bravo, Eline!' Meanwhile Maisa waves a fan. So that Missy Eline won't get too hot.

'My sister should be happy with you', someone whispers into her ear suddenly. It's Master Walter, who has come to stand next to the piano. Maisa doesn't speak and goes on waving the fan.

'I would want you as my own slave, too, you know', Master Walter whispers.

Maisa stays silent. She didn't know what to say. But she thinks it's nice that Master Walter pays so much attention to her. Some time ago, when they were children, she'd had a bit of a crush on him. And all those feelings are coming back now. He used to be the big white brother who taught her to play marbles and to swim. Now he's the big white man who might teach her a lesson in love ...

Maisa can't sleep. She's been lying on her mat in front of Missy Eline's door for some time now. She turns from one side to the other. Her thoughts are all over the place. She thinks of Missy Eline. She thinks of Master Walter. And about what they've said.

Missy Eline had been angry with her brother. Because she noticed him whisper in Maisa's ear. But Master Walter only laughed at her anger. And then Missy Eline got angry with Maisa.

'Remember, you're mine', she' said to Maisa. 'All mine. I don't want you doing things for my brother.'

'No, Missy Eline', Maisa said. 'I only listen to you.'

When the party finished, Maisa had to help clean up. Missy Eline went to her room. Master Walter continued to whisper things to her.

'Meet me at the river', he said. 'Where we always swam, when we were children. I'll wait for you.'

'I can't, Master Walter', Maisa had answered.

'Missy Eline wants me to come up immediately, once I'm done here.'

'My jealous sis won't notice', Master Walter whispered. 'I'm counting on you, my beautiful Maisa.'

Maisa had only bowed her head and said nothing back.

Now she's lying on her mat, turning and turning. She hadn't gone to the river. Had that been the right decision, or not?

Maisa suddenly feels a hand on her arm. 'Come', a soft voice says. Master Walter pulls her up. Maisa could scream. But it wouldn't help. Everyone would come running. And she would be blamed for the disturbance. And besides ... she doesn't really want to scream. She would somewhat like to join master Walter.

# Saturday

The next morning Maisa is neatly back in front of Missy Eline's door. No one has noticed that she's been gone for half the night. Together with Master Walter at the river ... Together with Master Walter on the grass ... Maisa has heavenly dreams.

'Maisa, get up.' Kiesja shakes her daughter's arm.

Maisa sits up straight and rubs in her eyes.

'It was a lovely night, wasn't it, Mama Kiesja', Maisa says, beaming.

Kiesja looks at her daughter. She's noticed that Master Walter keeps hanging around her daughter. And that missy Eline isn't happy about it. She has warned her daughter herself. 'Watch out for yourself, Maisa', she has said a few times. 'Make sure you're never alone with a man, not even with Master Walter.'

Kiesja sighs when she sees her daughter's beaming face. 'You haven't looked out for yourself', she says.

'I have, Mama Kiesja', Maisa starts, but then she stops. She looks at the ground. 'I couldn't help it', she whispers. 'Master Walter came to get me.'

Kiesja puts her finger to her lips. 'Come with me to the kitchen', she says. 'Then you can help me with breakfast',

A few hours later the family is having breakfast. The master, the mistress, Missy Eline and Master Walter. Maisa and her mother have laid out everything nicely. And now they're waiting in the kitchen until they are called on.

'It was a lovely reception yesterday', they hear Master Walter say. 'Thank you, Father.'

'You are welcome, son.' Master answers. 'We all enjoyed it. Didn't we?'

'Definitely', the mistress says.

Missy Eline says nothing.

'Did you not enjoy it, Eline?' Master asks. 'You must have done, surely? You were wearing such a beautiful new dress!'

'Yes, Father', Missy Eline says softly. 'It was a lovely reception. But I wasn't too pleased with Maisa.'

Maisa and her mother hear every word. They look at each other with wide eyes.

'What happened, dear?' Master asks.

'She paid more attention to my brother than to me', Missy Eline answers.

'Is this true, Walter?' Master asks.

'Well, you know how it goes ...', Master Walter says. 'We always used to play together as children. I liked seeing her again and we talked a little. Nothing special.'

'That's not true', Missy Eline says, loudly now. 'You took my slave. I looked like a fool. All the guests saw that she was just looking at you. And that she paid no attention to me.'

Maisa's eyes start to fill with tears.

'It's not true, Mama Kiesja', she whispers. 'It really isn't.'

Kiesja strokes her daughter's hair. She says nothing, but Maisa feels her hand shaking.

'What nonsense, sis.' they hear Master Walter say. 'Maisa was by your side the whole time. She was waving your fan for you the whole evening. It wasn't until you went to bed that I talked to her.'

'What?' Missy Eline shouts now. 'What did you just say? I ordered Maisa to lie in front of my door. I told her not to do anything with you. And she still did? I shall have her beaten at once!'

'Calm down, dear', Master says. 'It really isn't all that bad.'

'It is that bad', Missy Eline says.

Maisa and Kiesja hear Missy Eline burst into tears.

'Oh, child', the mistress says reassuringly. 'Stop crying. Just have something to eat and then call Maisa to you. She's always been a good slave to you. It's not necessary to have her beaten. I'm sure Maisa won't do it again.'

But Missy Eline is determined. She won't let her father, mother or brother talk her out of it.

'She's my slave', she keeps saying. 'I'm allowed to do with her what I want.'

'Well', Master says eventually. 'I would like to continue my breakfast quietly now. You can do as you please once we've finished eating.'

In the evening Maisa lies sobbing on her mat in the hut. Shani and Kiesja have salved her back. But the pain remains. Especially the pain in her heart.

'I felt so happy', Maisa cries. 'And now that's gone forever. Yesterday evening the world was so beautiful. And now there's nothing left of it. What should I do now, Nana Shani? What should I do, Mama Kiesja?'

The two women caress Maisa's shoulders and back. They stroke her hair. They don't say a word. There's nothing to say.

'If you ever get pregnant with my brother, I'll take your child from you', Missy Eline had said during the beating. 'Then I'll put it in a wooden barrel and let it float down the river. Because my slave should only pay attention to me. And not to a child. And most certainly not to a child of my brother'.

Maisa didn't scream when the whip hit her back. And she didn't cry when Missy Eline uttered her harsh words. I'll be home tonight, in our hut, she thought. I can cry tonight. There'll be arms to comfort me. I'll be safe with my family. Then I'll be taken care of.

Of course Shani and Kiesja take care of poor Maisa. Of course she is comforted. But Maisa soon enough notices that she's not the only one with sadness. Her mother and grandmother are sad too. About her. But even more about Kwasi, who hasn't come home since yesterday.

# Sunday

Shani walks beside the river. She comes here often to pick her herbs. But this time she's not looking for herbs. She's looking for the big yellow fruit that can end pregnancies. For Maisa, her granddaughter.

Maybe she won't need the fruit. But she'd better look for it now. The fruit stays edible for a while.

At a nice spot under a green tree she stops. She picks a large leaf off the tree. She sprinkles some herbs over it. Carefully she places the leaf on the water.

'This is for you, Diallo', she sings. 'Listen to me, from the other world.' The leaf slowly starts to rock. Then it floats from the side to the middle of the river. Shani smiles. Diallo has heard her. 'I wanted to come to you today, my love', she whispers. 'But my time hasn't come yet. My children need me. If you can, take care of my grandchildren. Bring peace into their hearts. And when my time has come, we'll see each other again. Then we will be happy in a better world.'

# Glossary

Page 13 : **Fire stick**
A fire stick is a gun.

Page 18: **Grease lamp**
A lamp made of iron or brass that burns oil.

Page 19: **Planter**
A planter is the owner of a plantation. Plantations grow coffee, cotton, tobacco, or sugar cane.

Page 21: **Gashes**
Deep cuts.

Page 27: **Tarantula**
A big spider with hair on his legs.

Page 30: **Cassave**
Cassave is a tropical crop. It is still part of the basic diet for many people around the world.

Page 31: **Tajer**
Tajer is an edible plant.

Page 37: **Disobedient**

When someone doesn't follow up orders.

Page 56: **Divan**

A divan is a type of sofa bed.

Page 66: ***...a burning hot iron onto her back...***

Slaves were branded, so that it was clear who they were. This happened on the ship, and again when they'd been sold to a plantation.